I Love Trains

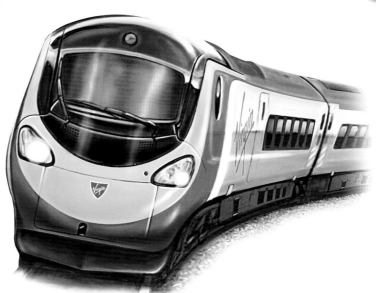

By Lisa Regan
Illustrated by Graham Berry

Miles Kelly

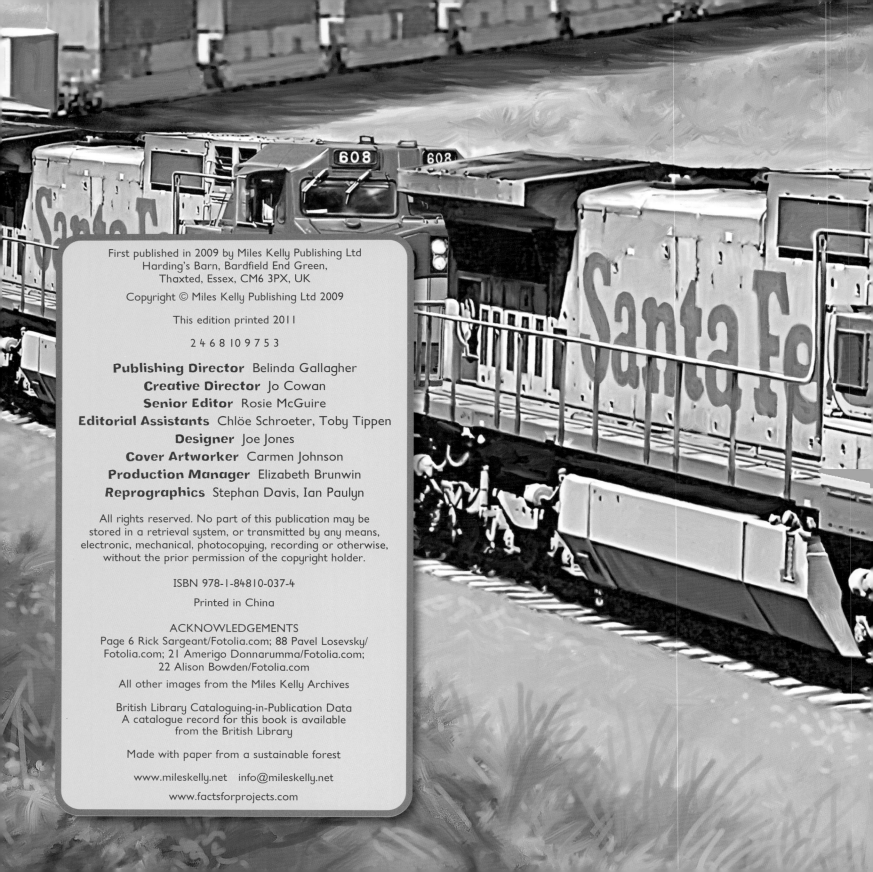

First published in 2009 by Miles Kelly Publishing Ltd
Harding's Barn, Bardfield End Green,
Thaxted, Essex, CM6 3PX, UK

Copyright © Miles Kelly Publishing Ltd 2009

This edition printed 2011

2 4 6 8 10 9 7 5 3

Publishing Director Belinda Gallagher
Creative Director Jo Cowan
Senior Editor Rosie McGuire
Editorial Assistants Chlöe Schroeter, Toby Tippen
Designer Joe Jones
Cover Artworker Carmen Johnson
Production Manager Elizabeth Brunwin
Reprographics Stephan Davis, Ian Paulyn

ISBN 978-1-84810-037-4

Printed in China

ACKNOWLEDGEMENTS
Page 6 Rick Sargeant/Fotolia.com; 88 Pavel Losevsky/
Fotolia.com; 21 Amerigo Donnarumma/Fotolia.com;
22 Alison Bowden/Fotolia.com

All other images from the Miles Kelly Archives

British Library Cataloguing-in-Publication Data
A catalogue record for this book is available
from the British Library

Made with paper from a sustainable forest

www.mileskelly.net   info@mileskelly.net

www.factsforprojects.com

Contents

Steam train

The first trains were powered by steam. Coal is burned in a fire inside the engine to heat water and make steam, just like boiling a kettle. The steam builds up and pushes pieces of machinery that make the wheels go round.

This train is called The Flying Scotsman and it still runs today. It has carried passengers for over 80 years.

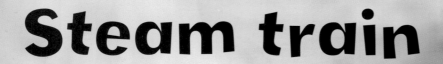

Freight train

Trains can carry huge loads. Freight trains carry goods such as coal and oil, and materials such as steel and timber. These things are called 'freight'. In big countries, trains carry more freight than passengers!

Heavy loads
Different types of container carry different kinds of freight. Tanker containers like this are used to transport oil and liquid gas.

Trains run on metal tracks. The tracks are joined to sleepers to keep them the right distance apart.

Freight trains can pull more than 100 trucks (wagons) at a time.

Goods are loaded into large boxes called containers to be transported. These containers are lifted onto the train by crane.

If the cargo is very heavy, more than one engine is used to give extra power.

Union Pacific Centennial

Huge, powerful locomotives (engines) are needed to pull heavy freight over difficult ground, such as mountains. In the Rocky Mountains in North America, a company called Union Pacific Railroad used the massive 'Centennial' locomotives to pull its trains.

Only one Centennial is still in use today. The others are in museums or have been scrapped.

The driver has levers and handles to make the train stop at stations and to control its speed.

The Centennial was the longest diesel locomotive ever built. It was 30 metres long – as long as a tennis court.

To get the power it needs, the Centennial has two engines.

UNION PACIFIC

6936

Maglev

This train uses magnets to glide along tracks. There is one set of magnets in the train, and another set running along the track. The two sets push away from (repel) each other, so the train glides above the track, held in place by the magnets.

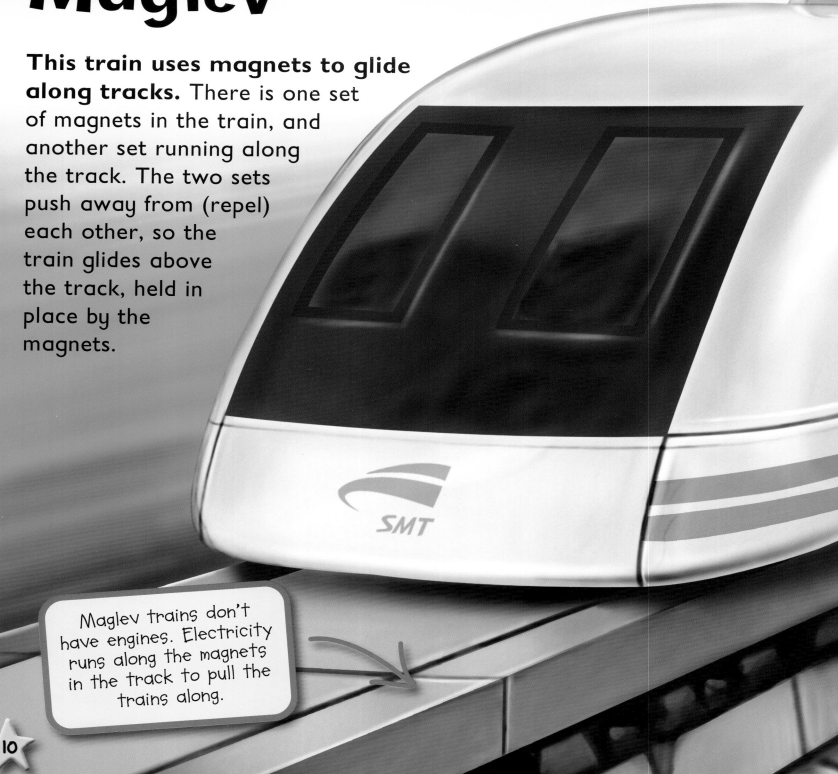

Maglev trains don't have engines. Electricity runs along the magnets in the track to pull the trains along.

Some maglevs don't have drivers. Computers make them stop and start, and control their speed.

Maglev trains don't touch the tracks, so their parts don't get worn down over time.

Feel the force

If you hold the ends of two magnets together you will be able to feel the same force that the maglev train uses to move along its tracks.

Superliner

This train has an upstairs and a downstairs!
Superliners travel all around the USA and parts of
Canada. They often carry passengers on very long
journeys, so there are beds and showers on board.

The upstairs compartments have bedrooms, dining areas and sightseeing lounges.

Double-decker

Having two levels – like a double-decker bus – allows Superliners to carry more passengers.

For an overnight trip, passengers can book bedrooms. Chairs can be converted into beds when it's time to go to sleep.

AMTRAK

TRANSITION SLEEPER 39031

TGV

This is the fastest wheeled passenger train in the world! It is from France, and its full name in French means 'train of great speed'. It usually travels on different tracks from other types of train, so that it can reach high speeds safely.

It is quicker, easier and safer to travel around France by TGV than by plane.

Speeding bullet

The second-fastest wheeled passenger train in the world is the Japanese 'bullet' train.

Some TGVs have two levels, to allow them to carry more passengers. There can be over 500 seats on a single train.

There is a locomotive (engine) at each end of the train, so it can easily go in either direction.

Most of the time, these trains run on special tracks, travelling at around 212 kilometres an hour.

Pendolino

This train isn't falling off its tracks – it is leaning to go round a bend. Being able to tilt like this allows it to travel much faster around corners than regular trains.

A sensor in the controls can tell when the train is on a bend, and makes the train lean to the side.

Pendolinos can reach speeds of 250 kilometres an hour.

Virgin

The name Pendolino comes from Italy where it means 'little pendulum'. The first Pendolino trains were tested there.

Twist and turn

The Pendolino leans into bends so that it can glide around them without slowing down – just like a motorbike rider does!

Trains are fitted on sets of wheels called 'bogies'. The train can tilt on the bogie without lifting off the track.

Underground

Many cities have underground railways. Passengers look for station signs on the streets, then make their way down to the platform in lifts, down stairs, or by escaltor. Below ground, they wait at a platform for their train to appear out of a tunnel.

Doors open automatically at stations. Trains usually only stop for a minute, so people have to hurry.

What a marvel
The Underground train system in Moscow, Russia, is famous for its beautiful stations and platforms.

The oldest underground train system is the London Underground, built over 140 years ago.

It can be hard to tell where you are underground! Big signs help people find their stations.

If no seats on the train are free, passengers stand up and hold onto railings inside the train for support.

19

Funicular

This train can travel easily up and down steep slopes! Two separate carriages travel in opposite directions. Both carriages are pulled by cables (ropes), which are joined together at the top of the slope. The weight of the carriage going downhill helps pull the other carriage uphill.

Most funicular carriages have big windows to let the passengers see the amazing views as they go up or down the mountain.

The two carriages often travel on the same track. The track splits in two in the middle to let the carriages pass safely.

Allmendh

Tram

This train travels on the road!
It is called a tram, and it runs on special tracks that are set into roads. Cars and people can use the roads around the tracks when there are no trams around.

Like buses, trams take people to the road or area written on the front. But unlike buses, they don't get stuck in traffic jams.

Green machines

Trams are powered by electricity, so they are much better for the environment than buses.

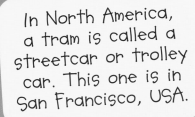

In North America, a tram is called a streetcar or trolley car. This one is in San Francisco, USA.

Most trams are powered by electricity from an overhead wire.

The San Francisco trams hook onto underground cables, which pull the cars along.

Fun facts

Steam train Since it was built, The Flying Scotsman has travelled over 3 million kilometres. That's the same as travelling 120 times around the world!

Freight train The biggest trains in the world are the freight trains used for mining in Australia.

Union Pacific Centennial The front of this train looks like a truck, with a windscreen and bumper.

Maglev The fastest Maglev can travel over half as fast as a jet plane!

Superliner Sightseer lounges in these trains let passengers watch the view whizzing by through a glass roof.

TGV A TGV reached 575 kilometres an hour in 2007 – that's five times faster than a car on a motorway.

Pendolino These trains are used in many European countries, and in China and Russia.

Underground The London Underground is nicknamed 'The Tube' because of the shape of its tunnels.

Funicular Many mountainous countries use funiculars, from Switzerland to Hong Kong and New Zealand to Wales.

Tram Trams have to travel at the same speed limit as other road vehicles, so they don't need to be able to go very fast.